# The Glassmaker's Daughter

Written by Dianne Hofmeyr

Illustrated by Jane Ray

For Niki and Jude Daly – D.H.
For my dear friend Sita Brahmachari, with love – J.R.

Brimming with creative inspiration, how-to projects, and useful information to enrich your everyday life, Quarto Knows is a favourite destination for those pursuing their interests and passions. Visit our site and dig deeper with our books into your area of interest: Quarto Creates, Quarto Cooks, Quarto Homes, Quarto Lives, Quarto Drives, Quarto Explores, Quarto Gifts, or Quarto Kids.

Text © 2017 Dianne Hofmeyr. Illustrations © 2017 Jane Ray.

First Published in 2017 by Frances Lincoln Children's Books,
an imprint of The Quarto Group.
The Old Brewery, 6 Blundell Street, London N7 9BH, United Kingdom.
T (0)20 7700 6700  F (0)20 7700 8066  www.QuartoKnows.com
This edition published 2018
The right of Jane Ray to be identified as the illustrator and Dianne Hofmeyr to be identified as the author of this work has been asserted by them in accordance with the Copyright, Designs and Patents Act, 1988 (United Kingdom).

A catalogue record for this book is available from the British Library.

ISBN 978-1-84780-677-2

Illustrated with watercolour, gouache and ink
Set in DeVinne BT
Published by Jenny Broom and Rachel Williams
Designed by Andrew Watson and Karissa Santos
Edited by Katie Cotton and Kate Davies
Production by Jenny Cundill and Kate O'Riordan

Manufactured in Guangdong, China [CC]

9 8 7 6 5 4 3 2 1

# The Glassmaker's Daughter

Written by Dianne Hofmeyr

Illustrated by Jane Ray

In Venice, recipes for making glass were kept closely guarded. A guild for glassmakers, the 'Ars Fiolaria', was started in 1224. Glassmakers became so important, they were allowed to carry swords and their daughters married into Venice's wealthiest families. But there was a catch – glassmakers were not allowed to leave the city in case their secret recipes were passed on to other cities and countries.

'Looking' glass was made by covering a flat sheet of glass with a thin layer of silver, mercury and tin – sometimes even with gold, which made the reflection more beautiful. There was a separate guild for looking-glass makers that made sure the recipe for making mirror remained secret.

There was once a beautiful city built on water.
Its palaces floated like birds in nests on the sea and
its lamplight danced like fireflies across the ripples.

Daniela, the glassmaker's daughter, lived in this shimmering city surrounded by delicate glass made in her father's furnace. Yet despite all this beauty, Daniela was a melancholy girl. She lay next to the canal all day long, scowling into the water – gloomy, glum and bored.

In despair her father announced, 'I'll give a glass palace to the person who can make my daughter smile.'

So his glass-blowers set to work. They blew
and pulled and pinched the molten glass into
silver-spun walls with pineapple-topped
turrets and winged-dragon doors.

News soon spread of the silver-spun
palace and people came from
far and wide to compete for
Daniela's smile.

First to arrive was
Maestro Barbagelata.
'Regard this!' he said as he blew
fiery rings of flame into the air.

He swallowed swords and even snakes and almost turned himself inside out with his tricks on a tightrope. But instead of exciting Daniela, she was gloomier than ever.

Then the most
famous of mask makers,
Donna Violetta Rufina Zangara,
arrived with a cabinet of masks – moons and stars and
suns, one a nest of twigs with tiny jewel-encrusted birds'
eggs, another a mermaid's lair lined with shells and pearls.

'Try these! They'll bring
a smile to your face,' said Donna Violetta
Rufina Zangara, holding up the smiliest of all her
masks. But instead of delighting Daniela, she
was glummer than ever.

Then Leonardo Leonino Grandi arrived. 'Behold this!' he cried.

He swept aside the curtain of his gondola. A HUGE lion jumped up with such a roar that the gondola rocked. Leonardi Leonini Grandi swayed… then fell backwards into the canal with an almighty splash, the lion on top of him.

But even this didn't bring a smile to Daniela's lips.

But one young glassmaker
longed more than anyone to make Daniela
smile. In a corner of the workshop, Angelo
drew a molten globe from the furnace and
blew a bubble of glass.
*'Flux and fire,'* he whispered.
Then he snipped the bubble and laid it flat
and smoothed on slivers of silver mercury.
*'Mercury and tin,'* he chanted.
Then he rubbed the slivers down
with a hare's paw.
*'Foiled and finished. And polished thin.'*
Then he sang his secret song again.

*'Flux and fire. Mercury and tin.
Foiled and finished. And polished thin.'*

The other glassmakers peered across at him.

'What are you making, Angelo?'

'A gift that will make Daniela smile.'

'She hasn't smiled for an alchemist, an acrobat, an opera singer or a sausage stringer – why should she smile for you?'

Angelo ignored them all and went looking for Daniela.
He held out his gift.

'Glass? I don't need glass!' She pushed it aside.

'Look again, Principessa. This is no ordinary piece of
glass. It's different. Look *into* it.'

Daniela scowled as she held it up to her face.

'What do you see?' Angelo asked.

'I see a creature with a mouth like an upside-down slice of lemon and the eyes of a cross dragon.'

'Look again.'

She peered back at the glass. 'It's the funniest face in the world.'

Then the face started to change.

The frown lines disappeared.

The eyes sparkled.

The mouth turned up.

Daniela burst out laughing.
And the more she looked at the person
in the glass, the more she laughed.
At each fresh peal of laughter, glass began to shiver
and tinkle around her.

The palace quivered.

A pineapple snapped off a turret and came tumbling down.

The silver-spun walls splintered.

There was a sound of CRACKING…

SHATTERING…

SPLINTERING…

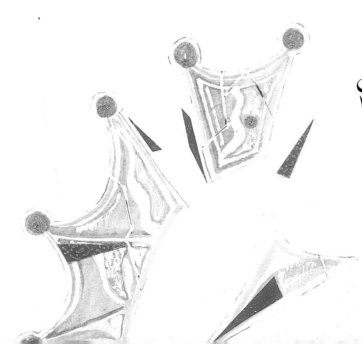

Then the entire palace fell to

SMITHEREENS.

Daniela's father rushed forward. 'Angelo, I'll build you another palace, but tell me your secret. How did your magic glass change my daughter?'

Angelo shook his head. 'She changed herself. My glass only reflects what's already there. Happiness is inside all of us. You only have to discover it.'

Daniela couldn't stop herself from peeping into the glass and laughing again. 'You're right. I found it by looking at my gloomy, grumpy face. I don't need mask makers, tart bakers, trumpet players, dragon slayers, bell ringers, or even sausage stringers to make me happy.'

And she laughed with such delight that the glass pieces at her feet started tinkling.

Then every bell in the city began to wobble with her laughter. The sound pealed out until even the palaces seemed to rock on their floating nests and all through the city people began to laugh and romp. Petticoats swirled. Corsets popped. Old men stomped.

Until even the Grand Doge came out of his palace to see what the fuss was about. When he heard Daniela's laughter, he kicked up his heels and danced.

So now when you hear the bells of Venice ringing out over the water, you can be sure Daniela is laughing. And don't be surprised if you peep into a looking glass to find a small smile creeping across your face.